A Southern Time CHRISTMAS

A Southern Time CHRISTMAS

By Robert Bernardini

Illustrated by James Rice

PELICAN PUBLISHING COMPANY
Gretna 1994

First Pelican edition, September 1991
Second printing, September 1994

Library of Congress Cataloging-in-Publication Data

Bernardini, Robert.
    A southern time Christmas / by Robert Bernardini; illustrated
by James Rice.
        p. cm.
    Summary: When a Southern farmer discovers an elf who has
fallen from Santa's sleigh, the elf tells him about Santa's annual
trip to the South.
    ISBN 0-88289-828-0
    [1. Elves—Fiction. 2. Santa Claus—Fiction. 3. Christmas—
Fiction. 4. Southern States—Fiction. 5. Stories in rhyme.]
I. Rice, James, 1934- ill. II. Title.
PZ8.3.B458So 1991
[E]—dc20   91-12467
                                                    CIP
                                                     AC

Printed in Singapore

Published by Pelican Publishing Company, Inc.
1101 Monroe Street, Gretna, Louisiana 70053

To all of us who love the South.

Here in the South where the sweet blossoms grow,
The Holiday Season comes rarely with snow.
The weather is mild, the sunshine is fine,
And we love our Christmas, a good Southern time.

So gather the young'uns and grown-up-ones too,
Sit back and relax, you can kick off your shoes,
And I'll tell you a tale full of down-home good cheer,
Of how Christmas works when it travels down here.

On a warm Christmas Eve just a few years ago,
I was out on my porchswing just taking things slow.
When all of a sudden a light struck my eye!
A red light so bright that it lit up the sky!

It flew to the left and it flew to the right,
And when it came closer it grew very bright.
In a flash and a scream it flew right overhead,
One second it stayed, then away! off it sped.

Well, I jumped off my seat when I heard something THUMP,
Out in the garden right next to the stump.
I said to myself, "Now what could that be?
What could that be that THUMPED near the old tree?"

My courage I mustered, with hardly a sound
I crept through my garden and looked all around.
And what did I find, to my big surprise?
A cute little elf, he was tall as my thigh!

He had straw-colored hair and bright rosy cheeks,
Tall pointed ears and cute little feet.
And his green overalls and little red cap,
Made him look like a Christmas toy freshly unwrapped!

Now just to be sure that this wasn't a dream,
I pinched myself hard, so hard I could scream!
Then I said to the elf, "Hey, what do you say?
Where are you from, did you lose your way?"

He looked up at me and said in despair,
"I fell off the sleigh as it flew through the air.
Flying so fast all the night long,
Sometimes it's hard just to hang on!"

My eyes opened wide, "Now could it be true?
Could it be true that you're one of his crew?"
"Yes, it is so," the little elf said,
"I'm a helper of Santa's, and my name is Jed."

"How lucky!" I cried, "I do declare!
To meet Jed the elf who fell from the air!
So tell me my friend, now what is it like
To fly with St. Nick on Christmas Eve night?"

"That's a secret," he said as he looked at the ground
And shuffled his feet on my cabbage patch mound.
"And it's never been told to a woman or man,
So I'd better not say for as long as I can."

"Of course," I said, "Jed, I can see what you mean.
And I realize that things sometimes ain't what they seem.
But I do have a question that won't ask too much,
So please let me ask if you're not in a rush."

Then we sat on the stump, me and Jed side by side.
And I saw he was sad by the look in his eye.
But I spoke not a word as I watched his expression,
Till he said with a sigh, "OK…ask me your question."

I replied with a smile, "I thought y'all wore
Big heavy coats and mittens and more.
But you're dressed like me, a true Southern man!
Now, Jed, tell me true, is that part of the plan?"

Well it must have been right, this question I asked,
'Cuz he picked up his head and his eyes lit up fast.
And I saw he was moved by some deep-seated pride,
And the answer would flow like a swift running tide.

"Sir, you are right!" he jumped, "you have hit
The nail on the head with your fine Southern wit!
Me and old Santa stay bundled up tight
When we're flying up north on Christmas Eve night.

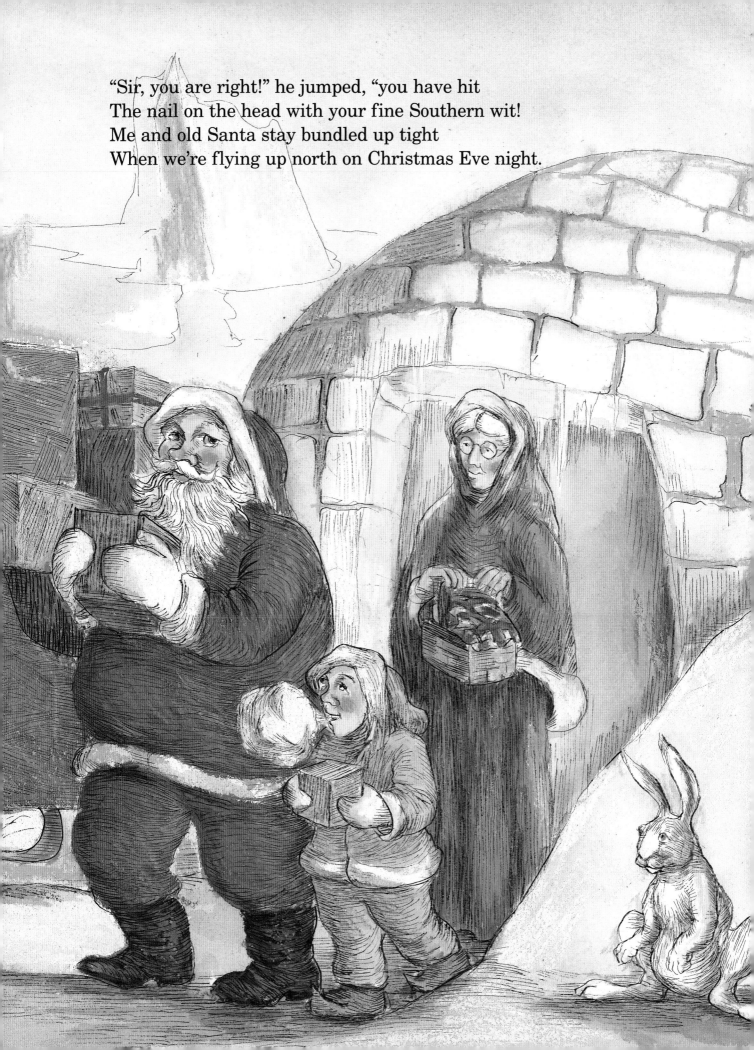

But once we fly over the Mason and Dixon,
Once we cross over that line we get fixin'
To taking off coats and sweaters and such,
And wearing these overalls we love so much!

We take off our scarves and our stocking caps,
We take off our mittens and then start to clap!
'Cuz Santa and I are so glad to be here,
So we can spread joy, and good Southern cheer!

We fly on due South, as fast as we may,
As Rudolf's red nose lights up the way.
We fly fast as light, we have to you see,
The whole South is waiting for Santa and me!

We visit the cities, the towns and the farms,
And each different place has its own special charm.
We fly over backwoods and big fields of cotton,
Beaches and bayous, not one place forgotten!

And in every house, and in every dwelling,
Santa leaves presents without ever telling.
But if there's a chimney too small for St. Nick,
I will squeeze through 'cuz I'm small and I'm quick!

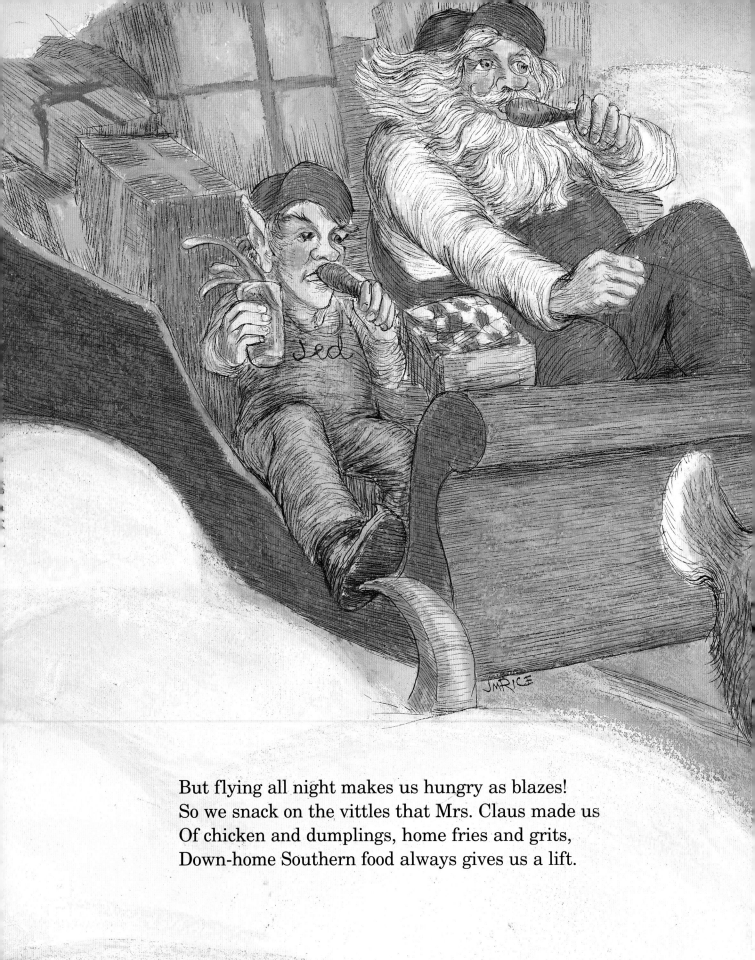

But flying all night makes us hungry as blazes!
So we snack on the vittles that Mrs. Claus made us
Of chicken and dumplings, home fries and grits,
Down-home Southern food always gives us a lift.

But tonight as I finished my glass of iced tea,
Santa turned sharply without warning me!
I slid off my seat and fell from the sleigh,
And before I could yell he was far, far away!"

Well, that's what he told me, this little elf Jed.
And I listened real closely and nodded my head.
Then I saw a small tear fall from his small elf eye,
And I thought for a moment that I too might cry.

Then I said, "Oh me Jed! I'm real sorry you fell!
How can I help, can I give Nick a yell?"
"If you think it might help," he sighed, "but I fear
That Santa is probably too far to hear."

Well I puffed up my chest and with all of my might
I yelled "SANTA COME BACK HERE, COME BACK
     HERE TONIGHT!"
And just as I finished this loud Southern roar,
I saw that red light streaking towards me once more.

They flew fast as light, in a blink they were here!
Santa, his sleigh, and those magic reindeer.
In midair they hovered a few feet away,
And Rudolf's red nose made it look bright as day!

Santa looked jolly, alive and alert,
In his red overalls, red cap, and white shirt.
The sleigh was deep red and the reindeer were gray,
And from that big sleigh old St. Nicholas waved.

Santa yelled, "Ho there! We've found our elf Jed!
Climb up here my boy and we'll speed on ahead.
But before we fly off I must thank our friend for
Signalling me with his loud Southern roar.

For I had no idea which way I should go,
But this fine Southern gent and his yell let me know!
You should be proud of your true Southern ways,
And I hope we will meet again one of these days."

Then he gave me a nod and a wink of his eye,
And he pulled on the reins for the reindeer to fly,
And I heard him call out as they flew out of sight,
"Merry Christmas y'all, to y'all a good night!"